Mrs. Peppel's
Pillows

Mary Flynn

ILLUSTRATED BY RENEÉ BROCA

For information See:
Author site: *www.MaryFlynnWrites.com*

This book is a work of fiction. Names, characters, places, incidents, organizations, and dialogue in this novel are products of the author's imagination or are used fictitiously. Any resemblance to actual events or locales or persons living or dead is entirely coincidental.

Cover art and illustrations by: Reneé Broca
Cover Design by Michael Butler of Torque Creative LLC.
www.MichaelbyDesign.com

ISBN: 978-1-7328380-8-6

DEDICATION

For my Mother,
who read to me each night.

Other books by Mary Flynn

— FICTION —

Margaret Ferry
Wishbones and Other Short Stories
The Flower Cottage

— POETRY —

As One Delighted

— NON-FICTION —

Disney's "Secret Sauce"
The Little-Known Factor Behind...
The Business World's Most Legendary Leadership

— CHILDREN'S —

Reggie & Rocky
The Ring-tailed Raccoons

Reggie & Rocky
The Naughty Raccoons

— MIDDLE GRADE —

Mrs. Peppel's Pillows

Other Published Works

The Saturday Evening Post Anthology of
Great American Short Fiction

14th Annual Writer's Digest
Short Story Competition Collection

Chapter One

"SHE'S WEIRD, LACEY. That's all there is to it. And weird people can be dangerous."

"Oh, quit it, Regina. She's not weird and she's not dangerous. She's just a little different."

It was a warm summer afternoon, and the two had stopped for sodas at Ronnie's Diner after leaving Mrs. Peppel's Pillow Shop.

"A little different? She puts a saucer of milk in front of a statue of a cat."

"It's her door stop."

"Oh, that makes it okay then – a saucer of milk in front of a door stop."

Lacey kept a light tone in her voice, trying to keep from getting angry. "I'm sure Mrs. Peppel has a good reason for everything she does."

"Yeah right. Tommy Sanchez saw her walking a peacock

on a leash. Who walks a peacock? Who even has a peacock?"

"Tommy Sanchez is a big troublemaker. You only listen to him because you have a crush on him." Lacey hated having disagreements with Regina, but the older they got the more they saw things differently. Regina was quick to decide that anything she didn't know or understand must be weird. This was sometimes hard on their friendship, but they had been best friends from the time they started school. So now, in seventh grade, they were more like two sisters arguing.

"What's wrong with walking a peacock anyway?" Lacey asked. "You wouldn't think it was odd if someone walked around with a parrot on their shoulder."

"Well, what about Andrea's mom? She was in the pillow shop one day and Mrs. Peppel came out from the back room wearing gloves made out of bird feathers. Bird feathers? Give me a break. I'm telling you she's an oddball. For all we know, she's crazy – so I don't know why you always go there."

"Lots of people go there," said Lacey. "And maybe I like crazy oddballs. I like *you*, don't I?"

Regina whacked Lacey on the arm with her cap. "Well, one of these days you'll find out, and just remember I told you so."

Mrs. Peppel's Pillow Shop stood at the edge of the quaint little town of Barlemarry, where Lacey Medina and Regina Strobel had lived all their lives. The shop had the look of a storybook cottage, with its low sloping wood shingle roof, purple window shutters and red, arched door with fancy brass hinges. Inside, a rectangular skylight was set in the middle of the ceiling. It was the most unusual shop on Main Street – about as unusual as Mrs. Peppel herself.

Lacey loved going to Mrs. Peppel's. She found it as enchanting inside as out. The deep blue walls had glittery specks that reminded her of far-away stars twinkling in the dark night sky. Birch wood shelves, the color of toast, lined the walls, their front edges carved with tiny birds and flowers. Mr.

Peppel had built them many years earlier. Now there was only Mrs. Peppel.

Lacey enjoyed going from shelf to shelf, fingering the small carvings, as she looked at the pillows, all smooth to the touch in every color you could think of. There were large bed pillows and smaller pillows for a sofa or chair. Each year at Christmas, Lacey and her mom picked out a pillow for Lacey to give to a favorite teacher. The pillows were that special.

People often wondered what Mrs. Peppel used as filler for her pillows, but whenever they asked, she simply smiled and thanked them for liking them so much. They were not very fancy pillows. Lacey had seen the fancy kind with tassels, beads and buttons, but Mrs. Peppel's pillows were different.

They were simple pillows, every one of them edged in narrow piping braided like Lacey's dark brown hair. The only way Lacey could describe them was that they were just so cushy-mushy mounded round and soft – so easy, squeezy, pleasy to the touch. They were plain heavenly. Even Lacey's older brother, Jason, liked having one, and Jason never liked anything that anyone else in the family liked.

Regina was right. Mrs. Peppel was different, but to Lacey she was just special, like her pillows – not fancy, but comfortable to be around. No matter what Regina said, Lacey saw Mrs. Peppel as having a quiet, pleasant way about her, and she always took the time to talk to Lacey.

Mrs. Peppel asked Lacey about school and wanted to know if she had any pets. When Lacey told her about her golden retriever, George, Mrs. Peppel told her all about the Yorkshire terrier she had had for many years. His name was Ducky. She and Lacey liked sharing photos of George and Ducky and laughed about their antics. George had once gotten into the closet, tore open the entire supply of Girl Scout cookies and ate all of the Samoas. Ducky once jumped right into the middle of a pizza.

Lacey often gave Mrs. Peppel a hand arranging the pillows on the shelves. She thought how much fun it would be to help Mrs. Peppel make the pillows. One day, she asked.

Mrs. Peppel smiled. "That's a lovely idea, Lacey, but the pillows are…well…tricky to make."

"I could learn," said Lacey. "You could teach me."

"We'll see," said Mrs. Peppel, with that easy smile of hers.

"I'd love to know what you fill them with."

Mrs. Peppel winked, then whispered, "Perhaps one day you will."

Lacey's Dad had said that the boy who lived two houses down from them was quirky because he carried his little dog, Rudy, around in a bright red pail and rode his bike home from school with his books on his head. Nobody called him crazy. So, why should anyone think Mrs. Peppel was crazy? Quirky didn't have to mean crazy. Did it?

There was something else about Mrs. Peppel that people found odd. Each day, Mrs. Peppel locked up the shop, and left for a couple of hours. Sometimes she left early in the day, sometimes later. No one could figure out where she went or why. They would see her midnight blue truck headed out of town, but they knew she couldn't be going home because her cottage was in the opposite direction, near the town square. She couldn't be going for supplies because the stores were in the other direction, as well.

There was nothing out that way except the old abandoned bell tower that stood high atop one of the distant hills. Other than that, as far as the eye could see, there were only country roads winding through the woods and, beyond that, green hills and endless sky. Lacey had asked Mrs. Peppel about it, but all she got in reply was that sweet familiar smile. One day, Lacey's curiosity got the better of her and she decided to find out for herself.

Mrs. Peppel always parked her pick-up truck around back of the shop. Lacey hid her bike in the bushes and watched from behind one of the big maples. It was a beautiful summer day with a deep blue sky and great puffy white clouds. The birds chirped loudly and the trees were the greenest she had ever seen them. Lacey waited and waited. Finally, about mid-morning, Mrs. Peppel came out, locked up the shop, and drove off.

As soon as the truck turned out of the driveway, Lacey jumped on her bike. She was careful not to follow too closely; she didn't want Mrs. Peppel to see her. Once on the country road, Lacey tried to stay just one curve behind Mrs. Peppel. But very soon, it was just too hard to keep up.

Lacey was disappointed, but she knew Mrs. Peppel would be returning in a couple of hours. She decided to wait at the library, a favorite place of hers. She loved to read and she always ran into people she knew there.

The butterfly books were her favorites. She could see the same vivid images on the computer, but she loved the sound of the large pages with their crisp turning, and the feel of the thick glossy paper.

There were so many interesting butterfly species with wonderful names like Zebra Longwing, Mocker Swallowtail, Cloudless Sulphur, and Common Birdwing. There was even one with a girl's name, Doris. And, of course, the most well known butterfly of all, the Monarch. Lacey's favorite butterfly names were Mourning Cloak and Great Spangled Fritillary. Such odd words. She loved odd words about as much as she loved butterflies. It caused her to be a slower reader than most because when she found words she liked, she read them again and repeated them in her mind. Some words seemed like music.

Lacey often watched the butterflies in her garden. They especially liked the perennials – Cosmos, Bachelor Button, Purple Cornflower, Milkweed, Zinnia, Aster and Black-eyed Susan.

"Butterfly books?" It was Regina in a voice much too loud for a library. "Are you kidding me? You're reading butterfly books? You said we could bike over to the park today. Some friend. I'm not making plans with you anymore."

Lacey had completely forgotten about her plans with Regina. Going to the park was one of their favorite things. If there were no young children around, they raced each other up the rope ladder and across the monkey bars.

"I'm so sorry," Lacey said. "I had to run an important errand."

"Well, you could have let me know. I waited over an hour."

"I am really sorry. Honest. It just slipped my mind."

"We can still go," said Regina, her tone suddenly softer.

Lacey wasn't sure what to say. She didn't want to lie. Her parents were very strict about that. Once, when Jason lied about his schoolwork, they wouldn't let him watch TV or go on the internet for two days.

"I'm doing something over at Mrs. Peppel's shop," Lacey finally said.

"The pillow store? Again? With that silly pillow lady?"

"She's not silly. I've asked her if she would teach me how to make the pillows." There was truth in what Lacey said. "I have to hurry now."

"What about tomorrow?" Regina asked.

"I'd better wait and see what happens today at Mrs. Peppel's." Lacey knew for sure that this was not a lie.

Chapter Two

A LITTLE AFTER noon, Lacey returned to Mrs. Peppel's shop. She went around back and sat behind the same big maple. The mulchy ground crackled under her as she got comfortably in place. She loved the maples and the sycamores with their canopy of huge leaves, like outspread hands.

She felt warm and sleepy and nearly dozed off before she heard the sound of a truck. Mrs. Peppel was pulling in. Lacey saw a large, light blue cloth sack in the back of the truck. It took up nearly half the truck bed. Lacey thought that such a large bag must be very heavy. She couldn't imagine what was in it or how Mrs. Peppel would handle it by herself.

As she watched, she was surprised to see that Mrs. Peppel effortlessly lifted the bag out of the truck with both hands and carried it through the back door of the shop where her workroom was.

Lacey had never seen Mrs. Peppel's workroom. As far as

she knew, no one had. Now was her chance. Once Mrs. Peppel was inside, Lacey slipped quietly across the yard to peek in the window. She ducked down carefully beneath the window and slowly lifted her head to see inside, but all she could see was a pane of glass painted in beautiful blue and gold swirls – nothing else. Lacey hurried back toward the trees to get her bike and head home.

All through dinner, she couldn't stop thinking about Mrs. Peppel and the blue bag.

"You're not eating your dinner," said Lacey's mom. "I hope you and Regina weren't into a lot of candy this afternoon."

"No, Mom. I promise," said Lacey. "I'm just not very hungry tonight."

She couldn't tell her parents what happened because she would have to admit she had been spying. "Spying is like lying," Lacey's Dad once said, "because you're not being truthful about where you are or what you're doing."

She couldn't tell her brother either because he would tattle on her. Jason would think it was fun for someone else in the family to get into trouble besides him. The more she thought about that afternoon, the more curious and determined she became. She had to find a way to follow Mrs. Peppel.

The next day, Lacey got a late start. It had been a rainy morning and the sky looked like an old gray lumpy quilt. When it began to clear, she headed into town. She hoped she hadn't missed Mrs. Peppel. She rode her bike past the front of the shop and noticed movement inside. Two women appeared to be making a purchase. One of them was Miss Gaitano, a woman she knew from church. The other was Mrs. Hollingsworth, her least favorite teacher.

Mrs. Hollingsworth had a reputation for knowing a lot but not being very nice to her students. She called Philip Runcey a dullard who shouldn't bother getting out of bed in the morning because the world wouldn't miss him. She told Alyson Chin there were gerbils smarter than she was. Even on happy, special occasions, she was sullen and critical. "Why on earth do we need all these silly balloons?" She would say.

When the two women emerged from the store, Lacey nodded to them politely. Only Miss Gaitano carried a bag, and Lacey heard Mrs. Hollingsworth say, "They're only pillows. I don't know what people get so excited about. No one even knows what they're filled with."

"You know, it's funny," said Miss Gaitano. "I once tried cutting open one of the seams but the thread was too strong. I never saw anything like it."

"I'm not surprised," said Mrs. Hollingsworth. "There's something about that Peppel woman that I don't like. I don't like her pillows either."

Lacey believed that Mrs. Hollingsworth would never admit to liking Mrs. Peppel's pillows anyway because Mrs. Hollingsworth's sister owned Carraway's gift shop. She, too, carried pillows, but she didn't sell many because people liked Mrs. Peppel's pillows better.

"Still, you must admit they are lovely," said Miss Gaitano.

"I'll admit no such thing," said Mrs. Hollingsworth. "That woman is strange. She has secrets. And mark my words—I will find out what they are."

Lacey didn't know what to make of Mrs. Hollingsworth's remarks, but the meanness in her tone gave her a shiver.

When the women were gone, Lacey went around back and hid her bike in the bushes, but this time she hurried to the rear of the truck and climbed in. The truck bed was empty except for a long rod with a white cloth sack at the end. Lacey knew Mrs. Peppel wouldn't find her there because she had not gone to the back of the truck before driving off the day before.

Lacey waited and waited. It was turning out to be a lovely day. The sky had brightened behind billowy white clouds and the great overhanging trees swayed slowly like the hammock in her Uncle Jesse's back yard. Here and there, she could see a bird leading her fledglings low across the sky, their little wings flapping as fast as they could. Lacey normally loved moments like this, time spent out in nature, peaceful and happy. But she was too nervous right now to feel happy. Did she really dare to go through with this?

She wished Regina could have come along, but her giggling would have given them away for sure. Lacey recalled the last time they hid under the stage in the school auditorium. It was the best secret hiding place in the whole school. They would go there during lunch and dress up in the costumes that were stored there. But Regina giggled so loudly that the janitor found them and brought them to the principal's office. No –

bringing Regina along was definitely not a good idea. Lacey was on her own.

Lacey heard the workroom door shut. Moments later, Mrs. Peppel climbed into the cab of the truck and drove off. Lacey had never ridden in the back of a truck. They weren't very far along before the ride became bumpy with no cushions or padding of any kind. It hurt being popped around on hard metal, and she was having trouble staying low so Mrs. Peppel wouldn't see her back there. On the curves, she was jostled sideways and had to grasp at a small opening in the bed wall, just big enough for a couple of her fingers.

She could see the town growing smaller as they went farther into the countryside. After a few more curves, the town was completely out of sight. The truck made a sharp left turn. A little later, it made a sharp right, then another left. Before long, Lacey could feel that they were headed up a long, steep hill.

The farther they drove the guiltier Lacey felt about spying, and the more fearful she became about getting into trouble. What if Mrs. Peppel found her there and was so angry that she never spoke to her again? What if, just this once, Mrs. Peppel didn't return to the store as she usually did and, for some reason, stayed away all night? Lacey's parents would call the police and say she was missing. She was suddenly very worried.

Lacey tried looking at her watch to see how long they had been driving, but the truck's rough movement made it impossible for her to read the time. It had to be at least half an hour. Lacey felt sore all over and was sure she would have black and blue marks from the ride. How would she explain them to her parents?

They were way up a long hill. Lacey held on tighter and dug her heels against the bed floor to keep from sliding out the tailgate. It sounded like the truck was working harder to climb. They were going very slowly now. Lacey couldn't see anything in front of them. Her only view was out the rear and sides of the truck.

The truck turned to the right and she felt as if they were going in a big circle. Suddenly, she was startled when the side of a stone building came into view. She looked up and up and even higher up. She had only seen this building in photos or from the far distance of town. It was the old bell tower.

Chapter Three

SLOWLY, THEY CONTINUED to circle the great looming structure, as the truck bobbed side to side over cracked pavement, loose stones and gravel. Lacey could see the overgrown landscape of ragged grass, weeds and untrimmed brambles. Arching tendrils of honeysuckle, myrtle and lorapetalum brushed the sides of the truck and Lacey had to duck deeper so she wouldn't be scratched. The warm afternoon air had a sweetness she had never smelled before. She loved nature's smells – the mossy fragrance of the woods, the milky scent of fresh cut grass or of a pinched boxwood leaf. Now, everywhere, the sound of birds, some she had never heard before.

What she noticed most was how very different the tower looked up close. From a distance, it had always appeared to be a tall, narrow, smooth white column, like a white candle rising from the far-off hilltop. But as they drove around it, she could see that it was much bigger than she had realized and it wasn't white at all. The stones were a light grayish tan color and they looked chunky and rough to the touch.

They had learned about the bell tower in class. It had been built more than two hundred years earlier by the Barlemarry settlers, the people who came to the area from the British Isles and established the town. These settlers were masters of stone masonry. They had constructed the old stone houses in and around town. Many people in the area still owned things they had built, such as stone yard benches, birdbaths and small statuary. Lacey's parents had always hoped to find something of theirs at an estate sale.

The old Barlemarry bell tower had contained a carillon, which played beautiful chimed music. People came from miles around and distant towns to attend the concerts that had been held there throughout the years. Lacey's Mom and Dad talked of concerts they had attended with friends and family long ago. People would bring their own chairs and sometimes a blanket on a cool evening to enjoy the music. When the new bell tower was built thirty miles away in Chestnut Springs, the bells were moved there and the old bell tower closed down. No one came here any longer; no one, that is, except Mrs. Peppel.

The truck slowed and suddenly Lacey felt even more nervous wondering how she could slip out without Mrs. Peppel seeing her. She was in luck. As soon as the truck came to a stop, Mrs. Peppel stepped out and made her way along the weedy path toward the building. Lacey quickly slid to the tailgate and dropped quietly to the ground. She scampered to the nearby bushes and watched as Mrs. Peppel went toward a heavy looking door made of dark wooden planks.

Near the center of the door was a black iron ring. Mrs. Peppel took hold of the ring with both hands and pulled open the door, creaky on its black iron hinges. Lacey watched as Mrs. Peppel walked back to the truck, removed the blue bag from the front seat, and took the pole with the cloth sack at one end from the truck bed. Then, she returned to the building and went in.

Lacey wasn't sure what to do. She was afraid that if she followed too closely or quickly, Mrs. Peppel would see her. On the other hand, if she waited too long, she might lose track of Mrs. Peppel inside the building. Lacey moved carefully toward the doorway and peeked into the darkness. The air inside was cool and musty smelling. A few tiny windows allowed enough light to come in for Lacey to see a large empty space and a spiral staircase in the center of it that went up through the ceiling.

In the quiet, Lacey could hear Mrs. Peppel's footsteps on the stairs and wondered how far up she would go. Lacey's heart was racing, but she decided to follow. At that moment, she had no way of knowing that the building was fourteen stories high and that Mrs. Peppel was headed all the way to the top.

Lacey climbed and climbed, stopping every now and then to catch her breath. The only time she had done much climbing was when she went hiking on one of her class trips. She had carried a backpack then, so she thought this should be easier, but it wasn't. From the occasional silence, she could tell that Mrs. Peppel also stopped for a brief rest. Still, it surprised her that Mrs. Peppel didn't seem to have any problem with all the steps. Mrs. Peppel was older than Lacey's mom, and Lacey had always thought that older people couldn't do this kind of thing. Maybe what her father said was right—if you stayed active and healthy, it wouldn't matter what age you were.

Lacey had no idea how much farther they would have to climb. She hoped Mrs. Peppel was not able to hear her steps or her heavy breathing. As she reached each floor, all she could see in the dimness was more wide empty space. Finally, after a few more floors, she could see faint shafts of sunlight coming in from above, and she no longer heard Mrs. Peppel. They had reached the top of the bell tower.

Lacey climbed the remaining turn of steps very slowly and ducked when she reached the final floor with its great circle of openings to the valley and hillside view beyond. In the center, she could see the thick overhead beams that once supported the structure that held the bells.

She stayed at eye level with the floor until she could see where Mrs. Peppel was. A small spider crawled toward her and she almost screeched, but with a wave of her hand, it went the other way. There was more light up there. Lacey could see thousands of bird feathers scattered across the floor, and nothing else except what looked like a small bench or footstool. She hoped she wouldn't start sneezing.

As she waited, silent and still, she heard a noise and turned slowly to see Mrs. Peppel standing outside at the low stone wall that circled the outermost edge of the top floor. She had the pole and the blue sack with her, but Lacey couldn't tell what she was doing.

Lacey crawled to the center of the dusty floor, where there was a platform just high enough for her to hide behind. It was right under the old bell beams, and she figured that it must have been where the bell-ringer once stood. She could see only a part of Mrs. Peppel's back. What on earth was she doing? Lacey wanted to get closer but was afraid. She turned and leaned low against the platform, trying to figure out what was happening and what to do next? All about her were bird feathers of every length, color and shape.

"Hello, Lacey," came Mrs. Peppel's voice.

Lacey jumped a mile. *Oh, no, no.* She stood up slowly, shameful about her own behavior. She didn't know what to say. Her face felt hot and throbbing. Her heart thumped heavily in her chest. She could hear it pounding in her ears. When she looked down, she saw that her clothes were disheveled and dirty from crawling on the floor. She wanted to die.

There was a long moment of silence.

Lacey's throat was dry as wood. "I'm sorry," was all she could say.

"What is it that you're sorry for?" Mrs. Peppel asked.

Lacey put her head down. "That I…that I…spied." It was a terrible word to say out loud. It reminded Lacey that the bad things you do seem even worse when you actually say them. What must Mrs. Peppel think? What would Lacey's Dad think? What would anyone think?

"Apology accepted," said Mrs. Peppel. "I think you just have a beautifully curious mind. You meant no harm, did you?"

"No, I didn't. Honest."

"I know." Mrs. Peppel's voice was calm and almost soothing. "But you can get hurt being alone in places you shouldn't be, especially when no one knows where you are."

"I guess I didn't think," said Lacey. It's what her mom and dad usually said when she did something really stupid—like the day she and Regina made flour crafts in the backyard and spilled a few pounds of flour in the grass. Lacey used the good vacuum cleaner to clean it up, clogged the machine and broke it. "An eleven-year-old should know better," her Dad had said.

"I've known you for a long time, Lacey," said Mrs. Peppel. "You're a bright girl with a kind heart. You appreciate the beauty of nature. I like that."

Lacey didn't know whether to feel better or worse.

"And what I really appreciate is that you didn't bring Regina along. Regina is a nice girl, too, but she has a way of disrupting things, hasn't she? Thank you for that."

Lacey was puzzled. "You mean you're not mad?"

"No, I'm not mad," said Mrs. Peppel, smiling. "Would you like to see the view?" Mrs. Peppel led the way out to the low stone wall. It was chest-high on Lacey, so there was no thought of falling off. And there they stood, silent. Lacey had never been in so quiet or so high a place. High above the rustling of trees, the flutter of butterflies and the scent of honeysuckle. Above trucks and roads and cars and buses. Above houses, stores, schools and libraries. Above horns and whistles, the squeal of children, the barking of dogs, and the teasing of older brothers. Above Regina's silliness and Mrs. Hollingsworth's sour look. Far above and far beyond everything.

A gray hawk soared past. Lacey could see its talons and its wide sweep of gray-white feathers. A swallow came after, then a flock of geese. Everything that was always so high up in the sky was now right there before them. A great puffy white cloud slowly drifted overhead in their direction. It was so close, Lacey was sure she could almost touch it. She felt as if her heart were dancing.

"We'd better get you back to town," said Mrs. Peppel. "You shouldn't be this far from home without your parents knowing."

"But you came here to do your work, didn't you?"

"I'll get it done another time."

"I'm sorry I got in the way," said Lacey.

They headed back down the long, winding wooden staircase. Mrs. Peppel carried the empty blue and white bags and Lacey carried the pole. Lacey thought they would never reach the bottom, but she was still in too much of a daze to care.

Chapter Four

ON THE RIDE back to town Lacey was much more comfortable sitting in the cab of the truck than in the back. But a question still burned in her mind – what was Mrs. Peppel doing? She was dying to ask, but was afraid to. Mrs. Peppel had already forgiven her once for intruding on her privacy. Maybe the question she wanted to ask would just be more prying.

"You're awfully quiet," said Mrs. Peppel. "Are you okay?"

Lacey looked over at Mrs. Peppel. "Can I ask you a question?"

"Yes, you may," said Mrs. Peppel.

Lacey was thinking of all those feathers. She remembered how light the blue bag was that Mrs. Peppel had lifted out of the truck the day before—"feather-weight."

"Were you…collecting feathers?" Lacey asked.

"There are quite a lot of them, aren't there?" Mrs. Peppel replied. "Had you ever seen so many?"

"Only in books," said Lacey.

"Did you notice all the shapes and colors?"

"Yes, they were beautiful," said Lacey. There were long dark gray-brown feathers, most likely from a falcon or a hawk. Some feathers were straight and others slightly curved, almost like a banana shape. Many were tipped in shades of blue, green, yellow, or red. And she was thinking of one little feather in particular. It was the smallest and most delicate of all the feathers. It was pure white and it had floated toward her, light as dust. There were hundreds like it scattered about. Lacey thought this was surely just the kind of feather that Mrs. Peppel would use in her pillows. One thing she knew – Mrs. Peppel had not answered her question.

"You're going to have to tell your parents what you did," said Mrs. Peppel. "You know that, don't you?"

Lacey had been so caught up in the moment that this had not occurred to her. How would she explain that she had hidden in the truck – that she had been sneaking around, spying on Mrs. Peppel.

"I'm going to be in a lot of trouble," Lacey said. Her face was flushed and her palms were sweaty just thinking about it.

"I'm taking you home. I'll help explain to your parents," said Mrs. Peppel. "But the fact is you did something your parents would never have approved of. I don't think they're going to be very happy with you."

Lacey was already imagining her punishment. They had grounded her for a week the time she left her bike unlocked outside the movie theater and the police found it in the woods with both tires missing, along with the seat and basket. This time she would probably get a month.

"Can't we just say I rode up with you? It's not exactly a lie."

"But it's not exactly the truth either, is it?" said Mrs. Peppel. "Besides, how could I ever explain taking you so far from home without asking your parents' permission? I would never do such a thing. No one should."

Mrs. Peppel was right, of course. On the way home, they picked up Lacey's bike from the bushes behind the shop. By the time they arrived at the house, it was nearly suppertime. Lacey's Mom was happy to see Mrs. Peppel and invited her to stay for dinner, but Mrs. Peppel graciously declined.

"I have some work to do for tomorrow," she said. She turned to look at Lacey and Lacey took it as a signal to explain what she had done.

When Lacey's mother heard the story, she wasn't at all pleased. Mrs. Peppel asked to speak privately with her and Lacey was sent up to her room.

"I hope you won't be too hard on her, Mrs. Medina. She's a lovely girl with a good heart and a bright imagination. And I do believe she has learned her lesson. She's very special. And the shop seems to fascinate her." Mrs. Peppel took a deep breath. "I wonder if you would let her help out at the shop now and then. Not a real job, of course – she's too young. But it would keep her busy with something she seems to be drawn to and, frankly, I would love to teach her. There are trade secrets, you know. So, I wouldn't want to teach just anyone."

"That's very kind of you, Mrs. Peppel," said Lacey's mother. "My husband and I will definitely think over what you've said. Do you go to the bell tower often?"

"Yes, I do. My husband and I used to go. We loved it there. The music was beautiful. My husband was a history buff. So he had the greatest appreciation for old architecture. The bell tower was built by people with a long history of building stone fortresses. It's a pretty sturdy old place. I didn't discover the very top of the tower until the place closed and my husband was gone. It holds special meaning for me now. You'll have to come along sometime."

Lacey's mother smiled. "I'd love to. Thanks. My husband and I have fond memories there, too. And from what Lacey said, it seems to be the best place for collecting feathers."

"Ah, yes, the feathers," Mrs. Peppel replied. "If it's feathers you're after, that is definitely the place."

"Will you be entering your pillows in the craft competition at the State Fair next month?"

"I hadn't thought about it," Mrs. Peppel said. "I'm not one for all that kind of attention."

"Well, I have a feeling Lacey will be hounding you to enter."

"I imagine she will," said Mrs. Peppel, a big smile on her face. "We'll see then, won't we?"

"I guess so. And thank you again for watching out for Lacey and for being such a good friend to her. I hope to see you again soon."

Lacey's punishment was that she could not watch TV or go into town for a whole week. Regina came over to hang out together, but Lacey never said a word about that afternoon at the bell tower, even when Regina asked where she had gotten the bruises on her arm. They were sitting on the floor in Lacey's bedroom.

"I bumped myself on something hard," was all Lacey said and turned the conversation to the upcoming fair. Outside of Christmas, the State Fair was the most exciting time of all and the biggest thing all summer.

Every year around the Fourth of July, for as long as anyone could remember, the State Fair was held at the Barlemarry Fairgrounds. Thousands came for the food, the rides, the arcade games, and the sideshows. And, of course, the competitions. People from all over competed for the blue ribbon that came with having the best steer, pig, pickles, pie, barbecue, cake, chili or rose, as well as arts and crafts.

"Is your dad entering his barbecue again this year?" Lacey asked. Regina's dad entered every year and hadn't won yet. But everyone loved Mr. Strobel's barbecue just the same.

"Yup," said Regina. "He'll be there again. I can't wait."

"It'll be such fun," Lacey said. "Mr. Houseman is entering a new rose this year, and he'll probably win again. Miss Tinnery over at the library told me. She said he named it 'Bonneted

Lady." She also said that Hector Rodriguez is entering his steer through the 4H program at the high school. He's a junior now. She thinks he has a really good chance of winning, too."

"Wouldn't it be fun to enter something in a competition? And win? Can you imagine?" said Regina.

"I want Mrs. Peppel to enter her pillows," Lacey said. "I bet she'd get a blue ribbon for arts and crafts. As soon as I'm allowed to go to town again, I'm going to stop by her shop and ask her."

"I just want to go on all the rides and see the sideshows," Regina said. "They have a new ride this year called the Sky-Shooter. It's like a sling shot. I can't wait to go on it."

Lacey shook her head. "Not me. I don't want to get sick. But I love the Camel Slide. That was my favorite last year."

George slowly entered the room, wagging his tail and sniffing for goodies. "Go away, George. Stop," said Lacey, and George plopped down at her side.

"Somebody said they're going to display a 5,000 pound bull."

Lacey laughed. "That's crazy. Bulls don't even get to 3,000 pounds let alone 5,000. Not a Holstein or an Angus or even those big Hereford or Brahman ones they use in the rodeo. I read about it at the library."

"How do you know they didn't feed it something special or maybe it's just a freak?" said Regina.

"Well, I'm not going to spend any of my allowance to find out," Lacey said.

"No, all you care about are those silly pillows and that crazy pillow lady."

"You shouldn't talk that way about Mrs. Peppel," said Lacey, with an edge in her voice. "She's a very nice person and very special, too."

"She's a very nice person and very special, too," Regina mimicked.

Lacey threw a slipper at Regina, and George pounced on Regina and the slipper. Then they all ate more cookies.

Chapter Five

LACEY HAD MISSED going into town. She missed the library and the Barlemarry Boutique, where she liked to look at the fancy, expensive grown-up clothes with their sequined tops, crystal buttons, velvet cuffs and such, the kind of things she would love to wear someday. She had missed talking to Mr. Flutey at the hardware store. He helped explain all the odd tools to her, the ones with the interesting names, like router and miter saw and cable thimble and dado blade. Her dad had lots of tools in the garage to fix things around the house. She liked to watch him work, but usually just got in his way.

She stopped by Ronnie's Diner for a soda, after which she bought some pretzel sticks at Weeks Market. The sun was warm and there was a sweet breeze as she made her way down Main Street past the lilac trees in the front yard of The French Café. The mid-day sun glimmered off the rooftops and silvered the trees. She was glad she decided to leave her bike at home and walk instead. And she was glad in a way that Regina hadn't felt like walking to town. Sometimes things were just more fun without her. This was Lacey's kind of day, filled with favorite places and people and interesting talk. She was especially excited to go to Mrs. Peppel's.

Before leaving the house, Lacey's mom told her what Mrs. Peppel had said about wanting Lacey to help out around the shop. Then she called Mrs. Peppel to give her permission.

"Thank you so much," said Lacey, when she got to Mrs. Peppel's. A couple of people had just left with their purchases. Mrs. Peppel was straightening the main counter area where the register was.

"I can't wait to learn about how you do everything." She'd been thinking about going back to the bell tower and working with those little white feathers that she hoped wouldn't make her sneeze all the time.

"I'm very glad your mom and dad agreed."

"Mom said I can also go back to the bell tower with you. She might come one day, too." A cuckoo crowed on the wall clock and little dancing figures came out of the clock's two tiny doors, twirled twice to the music and went back inside.

"I'd like that very much." Mrs. Peppel paused, then gently took Lacey by the shoulders. "You know, Lacey, I'll be sharing with you the secrets of my pillows. I'm relying on you to keep them secret. Your mom explained that too, right?" Mrs. Peppel's eyes were blue like the walls, with the tiniest specks of gold in them. They were gentle eyes, but deep, with a certain look about them that Lacey could only describe as a kind of knowing – a knowing look. And although the shop was cool, her gentle grip felt very warm.

"Yes." Lacey nodded. "And I know that means not even Regina."

"Not even Regina," Mrs. Peppel said, then added, "Especially not Regina." They both laughed.

"You're going to compete at the State Fair, aren't you?" Lacey asked.

"Oh, I don't think so, Lacey. I just don't like being so showy."

"Well, I thought about that, too, and I figure if I'm your helper, maybe you'd let me represent you at the fair."

Mrs. Peppel shook her head and smiled. "You certainly do think of everything, don't you?" She looked slowly about the shop. "Well, maybe we could give it a try, now that I have such a fine helper."

Lacey was so excited she could hardly catch her breath. "I'll be the best helper in the world."

Mrs. Peppel nodded. "Come on. I'll show you my workroom."

The door to the workroom was sometimes left open, but never enough for anyone to see inside. Mrs. Peppel was known to be a very private person. Lacey believed people made up things about her because they didn't really know her. Even Lacey would have to admit there was a sense of mystery about this dear woman.

Mrs. Peppel opened the door wide and they walked in. Lacey

stood breathless and slowly took in everything. It surprised her that there was so much to see. The room was neat and lovely, medium blue in color, its walls covered with the most beautiful framed photographs of trees and flowers, butterflies and birds, and tiny animals, the likes of which she had never seen. Lacey didn't know where to look first. The air smelled sweet and clean, like the dusting powder her grandmother used to keep in a fancy little pink box on her dresser.

In the middle of the room was a long wooden worktable with thick legs heavily carved with leaves, acorns and small pine cones. She had never seen such a table.

Around the room were wooden shelves stacked almost to the ceiling with fabric in many colors, patterns and soft textures. To one side was a sewing machine fixed in a heavy iron table stand that didn't look anything like her mom's or her Aunt Janie's sewing machine. It was bigger and heavier. In front of it was a midnight blue fabric chair with wheels, and on the opposite wall a deep, white porcelain sink that stood on four legs. To one side of the sink was a wall hook that held one of Mrs. Peppel's light blue smocks. There was also a tall set of shelves filled with large spools of thread to match every color of fabric. It was more thread than Lacey had ever seen in her entire life.

Toward one corner was the back door and next to it the window painted with the beautiful blue and gold swirls. Lacey walked over to the worktable and put her hand on it. It felt smooth as glass. On the table lay various scissors and other small tools and, sure enough, a very odd-looking pair of gloves made entirely of those same tiny white feathers she'd seen at the bell tower. The blue cloth bag rested on the table, empty.

Lacey turned to Mrs. Peppel. "Oh, I love it here. Thank you. Thank you."

"I'm glad you like it," said Mrs. Peppel.

"Where did you get all these pictures? They're so…so special."

"I had a feeling you would like them. They're actually photographs that my husband took."

"Mr. Peppel took these pictures? I never knew of anyone who could take pictures that good – personally, I mean."

"Mr. Peppel was a naturalist. He had the greatest appreciation, as I think you do, Lacey, for plants and creatures of all kinds, though he preferred the thrill of seeking out the tiny exotic ones that most people never see or even find. Take that one, for example – the one right behind you."

Lacey turned to see the picture of a tiny gerbil-like animal peeking out from between blades of grass.

"That's a harvest mouse, very rare to find or photograph." She turned and pointed to another. "That one is a Eurasian otter. And next to that a purple emperor butterfly. I know how much you love butterflies."

"Oh, Mrs. Peppel, I love them all – every one of them."

"Mr. Peppel would have been so pleased to hear you say that."

"And these gloves," said Lacey. "I never saw gloves made of

feathers."

"I have to use them when I handle the filler," she said. Then she sighed and folded her arms. "Well, then, the next time you come, we'll get busy putting together a few pieces for the fair."

"You mean it?" Lacey was so excited her voice almost cracked.

"I do," said Mrs. Peppel. "If we're going to enter, we'll have to get busy. The fair is only three weeks away."

"So, when I come back, will we go feather-picking again?"

Mrs. Peppel hesitated. "When you come back, the very first thing we'll do is talk about the feathers." She smiled. "Now go along and let me finish my work."

As they were leaving the workroom, Mrs. Peppel removed the light blue smock from the wall hook, and as she was putting it on, Lacey noticed a small silver frame embossed with a little heart. It was different from the other framed pictures. This one held a piece of paper—some kind of note—with creases where it had been folded, but Lacey wasn't close enough to read the handwriting.

When they were back in the shop area, Lacey thanked Mrs. Peppel again. There were a few white specks on her smock. Mrs. Peppel picked off each one very gingerly, held it up, and watched it slowly float up and out through the open skylight. Lacey wondered how she did that. Whenever Lacey picked lint off her own clothes, the lint just fell to the floor.

"See you soon again," said Mrs. Peppel.

All the rest of that day Lacey's mind buzzed with the excitement of being Mrs. Peppel's official helper. She'd seen the workroom with those unusual white feather gloves and all those amazing photographs of Mr. Peppel's. She and Mrs. Peppel would compete in the fair. It was almost too much to believe. But one thought more than any other came back to her over and over. She kept thinking about the lint on Mrs. Peppel's smock. How could it float straight up? She was puzzled by it and just couldn't wait until next time.

Chapter Six

LACEY LEFT MRS. Peppel's shop and headed back up Main Street toward the center of town. A car passed, beeping its horn at a cyclist, and Lacey remembered the quiet at the top of the bell tower. She couldn't wait to return there. When she came to Mrs. Carraway's Gift Shop, she saw that there were some new things in the window and decided to go inside.

Mrs. Carraway wasn't at all like her cranky sister, Mrs. Hollingsworth. She was a little timid, a bit of a nervous chatterbox with a high-pitched voice. Lacey imagined that Mrs. Hollingsworth bullied her when they were growing up. She probably hid her favorite toys and wouldn't let her have any candy. But her store was pretty, with rose wallpaper and glass shelves filled with every kind of small interesting item made even prettier and more brilliant by the spotlights in the pink colored ceiling.

There were swirly glass vases and picture frames of carved

wood, etched silver and ornate pewter. There were small cloth purses and fancy boxes of writing paper with matching pens, calendars and journals, coffee mugs and gag gifts, like the battery-operated singing gorilla Lacey bought for Jason last Christmas. There were tree ornaments and animal plaques and the most beautiful aprons she had ever seen, along with wonderful long-stem paper flowers, so intricate in their detail that they looked freshly cut from the garden.

Cinnamon candle fragrance filled the air. So many things to look at and, of course, there were the pillows. Mrs. Carraway called them accent pillows. They were nice, but not very easy, squeazy, pleasy to the touch.

Lacey had sometimes bought gifts here for her Mom or for a friend. For Regina's birthday, Lacey bought her a white cap that turned different colors and patterns in the sun. Too bad Regina's cat, Sophia, shredded it a week later.

Mrs. Carraway greeted Lacey with a soft smile. One customer was looking at photo albums, another was sniffing the scented candles.

"What have you been up to today, young lady?" Mrs. Carraway asked. "I haven't seen you in a while." Her voice was sweet in its way, but Lacey always felt that if her dog, George, had ever heard Mrs. Carraway's voice, he would cock his head the way he did whenever he heard something that sounded even a little shrill.

"I just came from Mrs. Peppel's Pillow Shop. I'm going to be helping her from now on."

"Oh, my, oh, my," said Mrs. Carraway. "Well, she must think an awful lot of you. She must, she must. And I can see why."

"We're good friends," said Lacey. "Next time I go, we'll be getting ready for the fair."

"Is Mrs. Peppel actually going to enter the competition? Is she? I can't imagine. I can't."

"Yes, she is."

"Well, wonder of wonders," said Mrs. Carraway. "In all my years, I have never known Mrs. Peppel to enter the fair. Not once. Not in all my years."

"Things are different now," said Lacey. "I guess all she needed was a good helper. Did you ever enter anything in the fair?"

"Oh, no." Mrs. Carraway shook her head. "No. I have often thought about giving it a try, not that I could ever imagine winning, but my sister, well, she just thinks it's all so silly. She doesn't think anything I make is worth entering."

"That's too bad, Mrs. Carraway. What kind of things do you make?"

"Oh, well, this and that. Aprons. Yes, I like making aprons."

Lacey thought about those beautiful aprons she had just seen on the racks and imagined that it would be very difficult for Mrs. Carraway's aprons to compete with something that special. Maybe for once Mrs. Hollingsworth was right.

"Maybe you've seen them," Mrs. Carraway said. "They're over there on one of the side racks."

Lacey's mouth almost fell open. "You mean those aprons near that side wall?"

"Yes. You saw them?"

"Saw them?" Said Lacey. "Oh, yes. Yes. They're the most beautiful aprons I've ever seen. My mother says so, too. She collects aprons from everywhere, but she always says those are the most special. I can't believe you made them. Why don't you ever tell anyone they're yours?"

"The paper flowers, too," said Mrs. Carraway. "Did you see those?"

Lacey turned and took a large blue and white paper peony from its rack. "You made this? You made all of these?"

"I did. I do. All the time," said Mrs. Carraway. "All the time. I sell a lot of them. Interior decorators buy them by the dozen."

"Oh, Mrs. Carraway, you must enter the fair. You have a gift. You do."

"I've never thought so," said Mrs. Carraway, almost matter-of-factly. "And, of course, Olive is so much better at sewing than I am."

"You mean Mrs. Hollingsworth?"

Mrs. Carraway laughed. "Oh, yes. She used to come over to my house all the time and use my machine. She made all of her daughter's beautiful dresses and..."

"Mrs. Hollingsworth has a daughter?" Lacey had no idea.

"Evelyn. A lovely girl." Mrs. Carraway sighed and shook her head, then dropped her voice to a whisper. "They haven't spoken in years. Oh, I'm saying too much."

"I just can't imagine what it would be like if my mother didn't speak to me for many years. How awful."

"Well, my sister can be very stubborn. She likes to have

her way. She wanted Evelyn to stay right here in Barlemarry. But after college, Evelyn took a job with a big hotel chain in Chicago and Olive never forgave her. Evelyn has tried mightily to mend things, but Olive won't have any of it."

"Wow, how sad," Lacey said. "What about Mrs. Hollingsworth's husband?"

"Poor Albert passed away when Evelyn was little. Olive had a rough time, as many single parents do, raising a child by herself. It seems she started blaming the whole world for everything that went wrong in her life. Silly, isn't it? You know, she doesn't come to my house anymore because she can't even get along with Nathan – my husband. Oh, I've said too much. Too much."

"Well, all I can say, Mrs. Carraway, is that you make beautiful things. They're special. And I think you ought to enter the fair."

Mrs. Carraway shrugged and gave Lacey a weak smile. "My sister would be…well…it just isn't worth it. But you're a sweet girl to say so and I thank you."

"Please just think about it, Mrs. Carraway."

The woman with the candles made her selection, paid and left, while Lacey continued to look at Mrs. Carraway's aprons and paper flowers. When the little bell over the front door jingled, Lacey looked up to see that someone was entering. It was Mrs. Hollingsworth. Lacey turned slightly, then took a step to the left, behind one of the upright racks. She was hoping that Mrs. Hollingsworth hadn't seen her. As Mrs. Hollingsworth walked to the counter, Lacey slowly made her way to the front door.

"Oh, goodbye now, Dear Lacey," Mrs. Carraway called out. "Thank you for coming in. Thank you."

Lacey reluctantly turned to say goodbye and found Mrs. Hollingsworth's cold eyes glaring at her across the room. "Goodbye, Mrs. Carraway," Lacey said.

"Oh, Lacey, Lacey," Mrs. Carraway called, "before you hurry off, tell my sister your good news. Tell her."

"And what might that be?" came Mrs. Hollingsworth's stern tone. "Or might I just assume it's more schoolgirl silliness."

"Oh, no, no, not at all," said Mrs. Carraway. "Not at all. Tell her, Lacey." Then she went on to say it herself. "Lacey is helping Mrs. Peppel enter her lovely pillows in the State Fair competition this year."

Lacey shrugged and stood silent. She was very uncomfortable around Mrs. Hollingsworth, especially since the last parent-teacher meeting, when Mrs. Hollingsworth complained to Lacey's parents that Lacey daydreamed in class. She went on and on about it, while Lacey sat quietly, embarrassed, wondering how her parents would react. They had talked about this at home when her grades were not what her parents had expected. Lacey had promised to do better and she did. On the last two report cards, her lowest grade was a B-.

Lacey's parents had listened to Mrs. Hollingsworth. Like everyone else, they knew she was especially rigid and unreasonable. Finally, Lacey's mother thanked Mrs.

Hollingsworth, then added, "With all due respect, Mrs. Hollingsworth, it might be good to remember that sometimes children may not care how much you know until they know how much you care."

Lacey's eyes had grown wide. She had never heard anyone speak to Mrs. Hollingsworth that way. It was almost like scolding. Mrs. Hollingsworth's posture became stiff. She put her head back, thanked them for coming and walked away. Lacey had never felt so proud of her mother, even though she did get a lecture on the way home about paying attention in class. Then they all went to Shiffmann's Ice Cream Parlor.

Now all Lacey wanted was to get out of Mrs. Carraway's shop.

"Well, I was right," said Mrs. Hollingsworth. "It is schoolgirl silliness."

She walked toward Lacey. "And it appears that your Mrs. Peppel is as silly as you are."

Lacey could feel herself getting angry. "What's silly about Mrs. Peppel entering her pillows?" She struggled to maintain a polite tone. "They're very special and everyone loves them. A lot of people love Mrs. Peppel, too."

"Well, we'll see just how special they are," said Mrs. Hollingsworth.

"I have to go," said Lacey. "Goodbye, Mrs. Carraway."

Lacey's father had taught her and Jason that they should never let one bad thing that happens in the course of a day spoil the whole day. He said they should always remember and honor all the other moments that held joy or laughter or learning of some kind. All the way home, Lacey tried her best to do that. She tried replacing the image of Mrs. Hollingsworth with her wonderful memory of what had happened earlier at Mrs. Peppel's. But it was hard. She just couldn't understand why someone had to be so mean. It made her feel bad. Mrs. Hollingsworth had a way of making everyone feel bad. Poor Mrs. Carraway.

When Lacey got home, she told her mom everything that had happened that day. She described Mrs. Peppel's workroom and talked about the State Fair. She talked about Mrs. Carraway's handmade aprons and paper blossoms. Lacey's mom was as astonished as Lacey had been to learn of Mrs. Carraway's special skill. Lacey also told her what Mrs. Hollingsworth had said.

"Why is she always so mean?" Lacey asked.

"I don't know, Honey," said Lacey's mom. "Many times people act mean because unhappy things happened to them and they never got over it, hurtful things that never healed. Things that might have happened years and years ago, even as far back as childhood."

"But Mrs. Carraway isn't mean and she's her sister."

"Well, look how different you and Jason are," said Lacey's mom.

Lacey shook her head. "Sometimes you just can't figure things out. They don't make any sense."

"Look at it this way. You're going on twelve and you're unhappy about the way Mrs. Hollingsworth treats you and others, right? Well, suppose that her bad behavior made you think that this is just the way teachers are. You might find yourself starting to dislike other teachers. Pretty soon, you'd start criticizing them to others. Each time you did, you'd feel angry. You'd feel a little angrier each time. If you got a poor grade on a test, you might blame the teacher. You'd get in the habit of criticizing and blaming."

Lacey nodded. She could understand how this might happen to someone.

"As you got older, your habit of criticizing and blaming might cause you to become cynical – you know, to always notice the negative side of things. Because of that, people might not want to be around you, and that would cause you to become even more cynical and angry. In truth, we should feel sorry for people like Mrs. Hollingsworth. She's carrying some kind of painful burden, and to top it off, she has turned people away from her."

"Mrs. Carraway said she got angry with her daughter, Evelyn, and doesn't speak to her anymore. I didn't even know she had a daughter."

"Well, that's very sad, Lacey. But that's what happens when we close both our minds and our hearts."

"Oh, Mom, I hope I never get that way. Or Regina either."

Lacey's mom put her arm around her. "I don't think you ever will. You have a good heart for others. That's what Mrs.

Peppel said, too, didn't she?"

"You know, Mom, I'd like to feel sorry for Mrs. Hollingsworth, but it's hard to."

"I know, Honey. And just because we do feel sorry for someone doesn't mean they don't have to take responsibility for their actions."

Lacey shook her head. "Life can be so complicated."

"All the more reason to be nice to people. People are one of the best support systems we have in life. Mrs. Hollingsworth has alienated so many people that she doesn't have anyone left to support her, except maybe her sister. Think about it. Think what it would be like if you had no one in your life you could count on to encourage you or be kind to you." Lacey would give that a lot of thought.

Chapter Seven

TWO DAYS LATER, Lacey returned to Mrs. Peppel's. The shop was busy, so Lacey asked if she could go into the workroom. Mrs. Peppel smiled and nodded. Once again, Lacey's heart skipped at being surrounded by so many amazing photographs and to think they were actually taken by Mrs. Peppel's husband.

Lacey walked slowly about the room. The blue bag sat on the workroom floor. It was still tied at the top and bulged with what Lacey guessed must be thousands and thousands of little white feathers. She was disappointed that she hadn't gotten to go back to the bell tower with Mrs. Peppel, but she knew there would be other times. After a few minutes, Lacey heard Mrs. Peppel saying goodbye. The little bell rang over the front door as the customers left. Then, Mrs. Peppel joined Lacey in the workroom.

"It's so beautiful here," Lacey said.

"I feel the same way." Mrs. Peppel smiled and sighed. "I'm

glad you like it, too. Now I think we ought to get started, don't you?"

"Oh, yes. Yes."

Mrs. Peppel walked over to the blue bag. "I was able to collect what I needed yesterday afternoon, so we've got plenty to work with today. After those last customers left, I put the sign in the window that I would re-open in two hours. And I think for today I'll just explain…well… how I get started."

"I can't wait," said Lacey.

"You see that I've cut and sewn these large squares." Mrs. Peppel gestured to the table where three empty pillow casings lay. One was a deep burgundy color, one a rich, warm brown, and one forest green, Lacey's favorite color. "This is usually where I start when I'm ready to put a pillow together."

Lacey stood near the blue bag. "Should we open it now?"

"Well," said Mrs. Peppel, "we need to talk about the blue bag and the feathers."

"Oh, I'll be very careful with the feathers. I promise to always be careful with everything."

"I know you will. That's one reason I'm so happy to have you as my helper."

Just hearing the words "my helper" gave Lacey a tingle. Here was the most special shopkeeper in all of Barlemarry and Lacey was actually her helper.

"Lacey, remember the day we were at the bell tower?"

Lacey nodded. How could she ever forget.

"You remember that the floor was covered with feathers."

Lacey chuckled. "Oh, yes, thousands and thousands of them. I never saw so many feathers, and so many different kinds. I thought what a perfect place to collect them, especially the tiny little white ones. They're the ones you make the feather gloves with, aren't they."

"Yes, they are." Mrs. Peppel put her hand on Lacey's shoulder. "But that's all I use them for."

Lacey gave her a puzzled look.

"What I mean is—I don't go to the bell tower to collect feathers for my pillows."

Lacey looked up at the face framed with soft waves of light brown and silver hair that fell just below Mrs. Peppel's ears. Now and then, the light caught a hint of reddish brown. Her eyes were deep and kind.

"Well, where else could you go to collect so many feathers?"

"I'm not collecting feathers at all. Not from anywhere."

Lacey felt her brow crinkle up, the way it often did when she had a tough math or science problem to solve. "Well, how do you get them?"

"I don't," said Mrs. Peppel. "I don't use feathers for the pillows."

"Then what do you use, and why go all the way up there if you don't want the feathers?"

Mrs. Peppel's voice dropped almost to a whisper. "Lacey, I'm going to tell you something I have never told another soul."

Lacey felt her heart skip. She didn't know what to make of this.

"When Mr. Peppel passed away, I was all alone. I missed him terribly. We had never been separated. He had been sick a very long time and we had used up nearly all of our savings. I wasn't sure how I was going to make ends meet, or what kind of work I could get. I had been a homemaker and never actually held a paying job because I traveled with Mr. Peppel for his photography. I was good at sewing and cooking and gardening, but that was about all."

"Oh, Mrs. Peppel, I'm so sorry to hear that. You must have felt so sad and scared."

"Sad, yes. I missed my husband terribly. But I was never scared because I had faith. I just knew things would somehow be all right."

"But what did you do?" Lacey asked.

"Well, the oddest thing happened. It really was the oddest thing. I was emptying out the top drawer of the dresser where Mr. Peppel had kept his socks and handkerchiefs and things, and I came upon a little light blue envelope with my name written on it. It was Mr. Peppel's writing, but it took me by surprise because I had been in that drawer several times after he passed away and never saw that note. I couldn't imagine how it got there all of a sudden."

Lacey listened, wide-eyed. "What did it say?"

"You can go over there and read it." Mrs. Peppel pointed to the little note in the silver frame with the heart, the one that Lacey had been curious about her first time in the workroom.

Lacey walked over and bent closer to read the slightly faded black script.

Come with me to our place on high,
Your future will not pass you by,
It will be yours for the taking;
Reach, Dear Lovey, reach.
Your gifted hands will see you through
To do what only you will do,
With what is yours for the making.
Reach, Dear Lovey, reach.

Lacey took a moment and read it again, then gasped. "The place on high—the bell tower!"

"Yes, the bell tower."

"But what did it mean?" Lacey asked.

"I honestly had no idea at first. I couldn't even guess what any of it meant."

"What did you do?"

"Well, I drove up to the bell tower. I hadn't a clue what I was supposed to do when I got there. I had never been inside. No one ever went in. We all had sat around outside to listen to the music. But by now the bell tower had been abandoned a long time. I had no idea what to expect."

Lacey leaned in on the worktable, her chin in her hands. She had never heard such a story. "You weren't scared?"

"Oddly enough, no. To tell the truth the whole thing was all so curious and intriguing that there wasn't any room for fear."

Lacey took a deep breath and tried to imagine how she would feel in Mrs. Peppel's place.

"You know what a long drive it is out there and no one around. Everything overgrown." Mrs. Peppel continued. "Once I found the door, I had to really work to get it open. Then, when I finally got inside, it was smelly and musty and only that small spill of light, the same as you saw. I had a flashlight with me, but I had to be careful using it because I thought that if someone from town saw the light, I wouldn't know how to explain things. So, I made my way in the very dim light, the way we did when you came along."

"Did you go all the way to the top?"

"Oh, yes. All the way, with no idea how high it was or how many steps."

"A whole lot," said Lacey, remembering. "I had to keep stopping to catch my breath."

"I did, too." Mrs. Peppel said. "I've gotten used to it now, but that first time, I just had no idea if I could make it to the top."

"What happened when you got up there?"

"Well, feathers everywhere, just like the day you were there. Like you, I thought they were all so beautiful." Mrs. Peppel shrugged and shook her head. "But what was I supposed to do? Mr. Peppel's words kept going through my head, 'Reach, Dear Lovey, Reach.' He always called me Lovey."

"He must have been a wonderful man," Lacey said, with a sigh and a faint smile.

"That he was, and very interesting, too. But most people probably thought he was a bit odd, the way they do me."

It surprised Lacey that Mrs. Peppel knew some people thought she was odd. "Well," said Lacey, "those would only be people who don't know you the way I do."

Mrs. Peppel smiled. "Thank you, Dear."

"So, what did the reaching part mean?"

"This was the most amazing part of all. I walked all about, looking up at the place where the bells had been, but what could I possibly be reaching for there?" She took a few steps, as if re-living the moment, then paused. "I went out to where the low wall is. I had waited for a beautiful day, so the sky was as blue as could be with big white puffy clouds." She looked off, as if seeing what she had seen that first time. "The view took my breath away, and as I stood there, a great white cloud floated slowly toward the bell tower. I just stood there silently, taking in the view." She turned to Lacey and dropped her voice to a deep whisper. "Then, I noticed that the cloud had stopped moving. It was right above my head, and it just stayed there. All the other clouds off in the distance continued to move, but not this one."

Lacey had heard so many stories of fantasy and mystery and magic, but she had never heard one like this and certainly not ever from real-life.

"I kept hearing Mr. Peppel's words in my head. 'Reach, Dear Lovey, reach.' So, I reached as high as I could. I reached toward that cloud. Sounds crazy, doesn't it? But it was the only sense I could make of the note. It seemed quite ridiculous to me. I reached, but just not high enough. I began looking everywhere for something to stand on. I started feeling a little frantic. I made my way downstairs as quickly as I could and found a small bench two floors down."

"I saw that bench," Lacey said with some excitement.

"Yes, it's still there, only I stopped using it, once I figured out a better way. But on that particular day, I dragged it up the stairs and out to the ledge."

"Was the cloud still there?"

"The cloud was still there and I stood on that little bench

and I reached up." Mrs. Peppel stopped, as if holding her breath, then slowly extended her right arm.

Lacey's eyes were large and fixed on Mrs. Peppel.

"And I touched that cloud, Lacey. I touched it."

Lacey gasped, then the two were silent for a long moment.

Finally, Mrs. Peppel turned to Lacey. "You must be thinking I'm as odd as everyone says."

Lacey shook her head. "Oh, no. I don't. I don't think you're odd at all. You had something so many people think about and even wish for, a magical experience. It was magic, Mrs. Peppel." In the back of her mind, Lacey knew that right about now, if Regina were here, she would run for her life."

"Oh, you don't know the half of it, Lacey."

"What happened next?"

"Well, once I touched it, I felt that I could draw it to me. When I pulled my hand back, the cloud followed. I made a wide circle with my hand and the cloud slowly circled with me. I was dumbstruck."

"What did it feel like?" Lacey's voice now had also softened to a whisper.

"It's hard to say." Mrs. Peppel motioned, as if trying to explain it using her hands. "It was soft…and…airy, but it had some sort of substance to it, as if I might be able to shape it or mold it."

Lacey slowly shook her head in wonder. "Shape or mold a cloud!"

"I really never felt anything like it. I stayed up there for a long time, but finally, I gently pushed my hands out, and the cloud drifted away. I didn't know what else to do. I went home."

"But you went back."

"Yes, I went back. Every day for two weeks, trying to figure it all out. Funny, but you know the porcelain cat I use as a door stop?"

Lacey nodded. The mysterious doorstop cat!

"My husband gave it to me many years ago. I actually named it. Seraphim. Well, one day while I was puzzling over all this cloud mystery, I walked past Seraphim and stubbed my toe. I laughed and said, right out loud to that cat, 'If I ever figure this thing out, I will give you a fresh saucer of milk every morning.'"

Lacey's heart danced with delight, remembering her words to Regina about there being a very good reason for whatever Mrs. Peppel does. She was so relieved to have been right, not for the sake of being right, but just knowing that Mrs. Peppel wasn't a crazy kook after all.

"Honestly, Lacey, it wasn't an hour later that it all came to me. I decided to sew a bag and put it on the end of a pole. I took another bag along, too. Like that blue one there. One bag to catch them, and one to carry them, and I took those clouds home with me."

Lacey tried to recall Mr. Peppel's words from the note, *Yours for the taking; yours for the making. Something that only you will do.* Lacey looked down in stunned silence at the blue bag.

Chapter Eight

MRS. PEPPEL LEANED forward and gently untied the white satin ribbon that held the bag closed. Then she took a step back. Large white puffs slowly floated out and up, gathering lightly along the workroom ceiling. Lacey watched wide-eyed. Her heart raced. She had never seen anything like it.

Mrs. Peppel gave a satisfied smile. "They're beautiful, aren't they?"

"Are they…are they…really…," Lacey could hardly get the word out. "Clouds?"

"Yes. They are."

"How is it possible? Nobody can do that. Nobody can capture a cloud, or put one in a bag. A whole bag full of clouds."

"Yet, there they are," said Mrs. Peppel.

Lacey stared at the ceiling. *It was true*. Now she understood how that white speck on Mrs. Peppel's smock had floated up and out through the skylight. It wasn't lint at all. It was a piece of cloud!

"But how did you know to make them into pillows? The note didn't say anything about that."

"Well, once I got the first bag home, I asked myself what I could possibly do with these wonderfully soft clouds. It came to me that people love soft things, and I thought of pillows. They were a little hard to handle at first. And that's when the feather glove idea came to me. I thought that the only living thing in the sky that touches a cloud is a bird. I gathered a bunch of those little white feathers and made the gloves. And suddenly the clouds were easy to work with. No one knows better than I do how crazy it all sounds."

"But it can't be crazy because it's true, Mrs. Peppel. This is the most amazing thing I have ever seen in my whole life."

"Now, you mustn't tell. That was our agreement," Mrs. Peppel reminded Lacey.

This was her very first grown-up secret. "I promise you, Mrs. Peppel, I will never tell a soul."

In the days that followed, Lacey was challenged in her promise. She was close to bursting with the wonder of Mrs. Peppel's story and her amazing cloud pillows. Over dinner, Lacey's mom and dad would ask how everything was going over at the shop and wanted to know how she was helping. Now that Lacey knew what Mrs. Peppel used as filler, they were curious, but they honored the agreement that Lacey had made with Mrs. Peppel that she mustn't tell anyone.

Jason tried to blackmail her into telling, not that he gave one lick about what the silly pillows were filled with, but it was a great opportunity to torment his sister.

"How about if I tell Mom and Dad that you got in trouble with the principal for hiding out under the stage floor at school. You and that mush-brain Regina. Did you think I wouldn't find out? I have friends, too, you know."

"Go ahead and tell," Lacey said. "That was almost a year ago, but it was only last month that you threw your retainer into the dumpster behind Ronnie's, then told Mom and Dad that George ate it." And that was the end of that.

Regina was not very happy about all the pillow goings-on. "We never get to hang out anymore. Some friend."

"It's only because I'm helping Mrs. Peppel get ready for the fair. When that's over, I'll have more time. We'll have the rest of the summer."

Mrs. Carraway finally decided to enter her paper blossoms in the fair. "You really encouraged me, Dear Lacey. You really did. Don't know if I'll win. Can't tell. Just can't tell. But I'll enter all the same and take my chances with the rest. My sister is not at all happy with my decision." Mrs. Carraway was the happiest Lacey had ever seen her.

Mrs. Hollingsworth remained as cranky as usual, but Lacey noticed that she came to town a lot more often. One week before the fair, she came to Mrs. Peppel's shop three times. Each time, she lingered a while looking at the pillows, but never bought anything.

"Mrs. Hollingsworth sure comes in a lot these days," Lacey said.

"Yes, she does," was Mrs. Peppel's quiet reply.

She had made Lacey her very own pair of feather gloves, which she used to help place the clouds into the cases that Mrs. Peppel cut. She showed Lacey how she stitched the pillow seams with what she called her "specialty thread" and bound them with her fine braided piping. Lacey and Mrs. Peppel knew they would have to dress up the pillows more than usual for the competition. They would pick out the most vibrant colors and unique patterns. They would braid more than one color together for the piping. They made a very good team.

One day, Lacey accompanied Mrs. Peppel back up to the bell tower. It was a beautiful clear day with a sky that had perfect white puffy clouds. This, she learned, was the reason Mrs. Peppel left town at all different times of the day—it had to be just the right kind of day with just the right kind of clouds. Sometimes the clouds were best in the morning, sometimes later in the day. And some days were not at all good cloud-picking days.

Mrs. Peppel taught Lacey that they could use only the large cumulus clouds, the big puffy white ones. The very first time Lacey drew one in, she nearly screeched in amazement. "This really is a most heavenly experience," she said, laughing.

"Truly," said Mrs. Peppel, and the two got on better than ever.

Lacey had learned about clouds in school. Stratus clouds were long, low flat clouds, cumulus were higher, big, white and puffy, like giant cotton balls, the kind Mrs. Peppel used. Cirrus clouds were the feathery kind. Nimbus clouds were the darker rain clouds, and cumulonimbus were the really dark scary ones that brought the thunderstorms. Lacey didn't like thunderstorms, but she loved the word "cumulonimbus." The first time she'd heard it, she said it over and over again. Cumulonimbus—such a neat word for such a scary force of nature.

The first thing that Lacey learned about the pillow clouds was never, never to collect the cumulonimbus kind. You would definitely not want to have those dark thunderstorm clouds captured up inside a pillow. "Believe me," said Mrs. Peppel, "it would not be pretty."

Lacey also learned that even though the cumulus clouds were puffy and white, they were always gray at the bottom. Lacey had to gently brush away the gray and send it floating off into the sky. All Mrs. Peppel wanted were pure white puffy clouds.

Lacey now had her very own equipment – a pole with a white sack attached at one end for bringing in the clouds, and her very own blue bag, the same as Mrs. Peppel's, except tied with a pink ribbon to tell them apart. This made it easier for Mrs. Peppel to inspect Lacey's work.

When the fair was barely two days away, Lacey visited Mrs. Carraway's shop to see how she was coming along with her paper blossom entries. Mrs. Carraway went to the back room and returned carrying a wide, flat basket filled with pink and white peonies, deep pink bearded lilies, and brilliant blue delphinius, all made of paper.

"I've never seen such beautiful flowers, except of course the real ones," Lacey said, shaking her head in wonder. "They are bound to win a prize."

"I'm glad you think so, Dear Lacey. My sister surely doesn't."

"You have a gift, Mrs. Carraway. Please don't let Mrs. Hollingsworth discourage you. She just doesn't care at all about the fair."

"Well," said Mrs. Carraway, dropping her voice to a whisper, "I'm so glad you came in today because I have a secret and you are the only person in the world I would ever tell. It may shock you as much as it did me."

Lacey wondered what on earth it could be.

"My sister is actually thinking about entering the competition. I wasn't supposed to tell anyone."

Lacey's mouth fell open. "Mrs. Hollingsworth is entering something at the fair?"

"She might be, yes." Mrs. Carraway looked around even though there was no one else in the store. "And you'll never guess in a hundred years what that something might be. Not in a hundred years."

"I can't imagine," Lacey whispered back.

Mrs. Carraway leaned close and whispered, "Pillows."

"Pillows?" Lacey blurted out.

"Oh, I should never have told. Never. If my sister finds out, she'll be furious."

"Pillows?" Lacey couldn't get past the idea of it.

"It's not a sure thing," said Mrs. Carraway. "Not sure at all. She's waiting for something, but I don't know what. I think my dear sister is up to, well, hanky-panky."

Lacey felt a shiver thinking of Mrs. Hollingsworth's recent visits to Mrs. Peppel's. She thanked Mrs. Carraway for telling her and hurried off.

When Lacey got to the pillow shop, she saw that Mrs. Peppel was preparing to lock up the store.

"Oh, good. I've been waiting for you. Would you like to take a ride?"

"Sure. Where to?" Lacey asked.

"I have a few errands to run. I thought you might like to tag along."

This was a neat surprise because it was the first time she would be going somewhere with Mrs. Peppel, other than the bell tower. "Oh, yes, I would love to come."

Mrs. Peppel locked the back door and as they climbed into the truck, Lacey saw that there was a cardboard carton on her side.

"Oh, do me a favor, Lacey, would you please. Put that carton by the back door. They're just some extra pillows I made up in case we needed them.

"I should put them inside, shouldn't I?"

"That's not necessary," said Mrs. Peppel. "Things are usually safe back here and we won't be gone very long."

Lacey told Mrs. Peppel about her conversation with Mrs. Carraway.

"How interesting". I'll bet Mrs. Hollingsworth will make some lovely pillows."

"Aren't you concerned?" Lacey asked. "Pillows? Hanky-panky? Look how many times Mrs. Hollingsworth has been here this week. What if she's up to something?"

Mrs. Peppel appeared to be cheerful and calm. "It's a

beautiful day and I don't think we should give it another thought."

Lacey took the carton, reluctantly set it outside the back door of the shop, and sighed. Mrs. Peppel usually knew best. Lacey hoped that this time would not be an exception.

Chapter Nine

LACEY CONTINUED TO feel troubled by what Mrs. Hollingsworth might be up to, but she didn't mention it again. Instead, she tried to be as happy as Mrs. Peppel, and was pleased to see how warmly people around town greeted the two of them. Lacey noticed that although many people thought Mrs. Peppel had odd ways, they were drawn to her warmth and gentle spirit.

Lacey and Mrs. Peppel stopped at the post office, the grocer, and the hardware store, where Mr. Flutey's fussing made Lacey feel proud.

"You've got a fine helper here, Abigail," Mr. Flutey said, gently tugging at the end of the long, ribboned braid that fell across Lacey's right shoulder. Lacey had never heard Mrs. Peppel called by her first name. Abigail. She thought the name suited Mrs. Peppel just fine.

"Indeed, I do, Samuel."

Samuel. Lacey had always heard Mr. Flutey called Sam by the people who shopped there, mostly men, but she thought Samuel was quite a nice name, too. Mr. Flutey was a fine man. Everyone said so. Tall and strong, smart and kind. Every year, he donated tools to Barlemarry High School for the students to use in shop class. At Christmas, he gave money to match people's donations for the less fortunate. He was always willing to help anyone who needed it. Mrs. Flutey had passed away years earlier. Lacey looked up at Mr. Flutey, then at Mrs. Peppel. *Wouldn't they make a nice couple?*

On the way back to the shop, they stopped by Schiffmann's Ice Cream Parlor where Mrs. Peppel treated Lacey to her favorite sundae, mint chocolate chip covered in warm marshmallow and topped with whipped cream and rainbow sprinkles. Lacey was happy that Mrs. Peppel had taken her along. It was a beautiful warm summer day and a fun time. But when they pulled around back of the shop, the mood quickly changed. The cardboard carton was gone.

Lacey's heart sank, but her unhappy surprise quickly mixed with anger. "I knew it. I just knew it. It's Mrs. Hollingsworth, I'm sure of it. She's been hanging around here all week. She's a mean, mean woman."

"If this is Mrs. Hollingsworth's doing, what do you suppose she'll do with the pillows?" Mrs. Peppel was surprisingly calm.

"I'll bet I know exactly what she'll do." Lacey's mouth had tightened into a thin line. "She'll open them up and find out your secret. Then she'll use the clouds to make her own pillows and enter them in the fair. Don't you see, Mrs. Peppel? This is what she was waiting for. She was waiting for a way to get your pillows."

"But why do you think she would steal them when she can buy them?"

"Because," said Lacey, "if she's entering pillows in the fair, she doesn't want people to know she has any of *your* pillows. They would realize she copied them or used them in some way to win. Oh, Mrs. Peppel, I'm so upset."

They sat for a quiet moment.

"Let's go inside, Lacey. There's something I want to show you."

When they opened the back door, the mid-afternoon

sun streaked across the worktable and the color caught in its brilliance was dazzling. Even at a time such as this, the splendor of this room fascinated Lacey. There was so much life, energy and beauty here. Still she slung herself onto the chair, head down.

"Have heart, Dear Lacey," said Mrs. Peppel, picking up one of the pillows they had made for the fair. "Come on over here," she said, placing it on the table.

"I'm sorry, Mrs. Peppel, but I just don't feel like a very good helper right now."

"Come, I need you to see this."

Lacey looked up. *See what*? She stood at the table.

"Now," said Mrs. Peppel, handing Lacey the scissors, "I want you to cut open this pillow."

Lacey couldn't believe what Mrs. Peppel had just told her to do. "You want me to cut open this pillow?" She asked, with a confused look on her face.

"That's right. Start with the seam. Just cut the threads." Mrs. Peppel was so calm and matter of fact, Lacey didn't know what to make of it.

"I don't think I can," said Lacey. "It's too beautiful. It's our work. It's for the fair."

"I know. But just go ahead. You'll see why in a moment."

Lacey tucked the scissor point into the seam and pulled. Then, she tried to make little cuttings along the stitch line. She picked and snipped and poked and pulled. "I'm sorry, Mrs. Peppel, it's not working. I don't seem to be able to do it." She recalled what Miss Gaitano had said about not being able to cut the thread.

"I know," said Mrs. Peppel. "That's because I used my specialty thread. Remember?"

"Well, what if she just tears it open?"

"Okay," said Mrs. Peppel. "Try this. Take the scissors and stick it right into the pillow. Go ahead. Just pierce the pillow with the point of the scissors."

Lacey found it very hard to follow Mrs. Peppel's orders. The pillows were so special. Still, she took the scissors and pressed the point against the pillow as hard as she could. Nothing. She pressed harder, leaning on it with all her might. Still nothing. She tried to make a slash mark. Nothing.

Lacey looked up at Mrs. Peppel, surprised. "Nothing happened. I can't do it."

"No one can," Mrs. Peppel said, with a twinkle in her eye.

All of this felt like more than Lacey's mind could hold. "What do you mean?"

"I mean just that. No one can cut open one of these pillows. Not anyone, not even Mrs. Hollingsworth. Not only that, but no one can handle the clouds either."

"But you were able to cut the fabric to make the pillows," Lacey said, still finding it hard to believe.

"I know," Mrs. Peppel said. "But once they're finished, no one can cut into them except me."

Lacey sat back down. This was just too much amazement. Everything about Mrs. Peppel was amazing. "Magic!" was all she could think of saying. She hated to use Regina's word, but it all did seem…well…crazy.

"So, you see. You needn't worry. Mrs. Hollingsworth will not be able to discover our cloud secret."

Lacey sighed. "Well, I'm sure glad about that. But she still has your pillows and I just don't trust her."

Mrs. Peppel patted Lacey's shoulder. "But you can trust me. Everything will be just fine."

Over supper, Lacey said nothing about what had happened. She would have to be careful not to explain too much. But she did tell about her trip through town with Mrs. Peppel and how she thought Mrs. Peppel and Mr. Flutey would make a nice couple. She thought "Abigail Flutey" made a lovely name, almost musical. She also talked about Mrs. Carraway's beautiful paper blossoms, all the time remembering what Mrs. Peppel had said about things turning out okay. Lacey wished more than anything that she could believe that. She had the most awful feeling.

Chapter Ten

OPENING DAY OF the State Fair was about as nice and sunny a day as anyone could have hoped for. Trees were their fullest green. Asters, cosmos, hollyhocks and snapdragons overflowed their beds and window boxes. The fragrant summer air was alive with chirps and buzzes and the flutter of wings.

Bright red and blue banners, pennants and bunting adorned buildings, store fronts, poles and windows all the way to the fairgrounds. The town bustled with the frantic activity of visitors in cars and on foot, along with the trailers and trucks used by the exhibitors and vendors. Six motor coaches rolled slowly through the crowded streets, carrying the headlining rock bands.

Regina, her mom, and eight-year-old brother, Troy, were busy helping Mr. Strobel with the preparations for the barbecue competition, something Regina always enjoyed. They had a trailer with a large black metal grill and enough slabs of Mr. Strobel's hand-rubbed ribs to feed a pride of lion for a year. They would arrive early so that the ribs could slow cook for many hours before the judging.

Lacey had missed Regina because of all the time spent at Mrs. Peppel's. It was too bad that she would never be able to share with her all her astonishing experiences with the clouds and the bell tower and the magic of the pillows.

The fair was to open officially at 11:00. Lacey had to be to Mrs. Peppel's by 8:30. Her dad drove her to town and since they were a little early, she asked him to drop her off at Mrs. Carraway's shop to check on her. She would catch up with her mom, dad and Jason later in the day at Mrs. Peppel's exhibit table. Lacey's excitement about the fair and the competition had mostly overshadowed her worries about Mrs. Hollingsworth. Of the pillows they had made for the competition, they had selected the three they thought were the prettiest and most eye-catching.

Lacey found Mrs. Carraway all a flutter with nerves and doubts. The basket of paper blossoms was set on the counter, ready to go. Lacey thought it was too bad that Mrs. Hollingsworth wouldn't help or support her sister instead of making trouble for others.

"These are definitely prize-winners, Mrs. Carraway."

"Oh, so nice of you to say, Lacey. So nice of you."

"I was hoping Mrs. Hollingsworth would help you."

"Heavens, no. But my husband will be here soon." She sighed deeply. "Olive has been working frantically on her own entries. And of all things, I have no idea why she would pick pillows, what with Mrs. Peppel entering. Who could compete with Mrs. Peppel's pillows?

Lacey's back stiffened. There was no doubt in her mind now that Mrs. Hollingsworth had taken the carton of pillows from the back of Mrs. Peppel's shop. But what could she do with them? She wouldn't be able to undo them in any way.

"What kind of pillows is she making?" Lacey asked. "Did you see them?"

"No. All I saw were the pillow covers. She came over to use my sewing machine. I was too busy in the shop to pay much attention."

"Well, I'd better get going," Lacey said. "Good luck to you, Mrs. Carraway." And off she went.

Lacey was breathless running to Mrs. Peppel's. She told Mrs. Peppel that Mrs. Hollingsworth was definitely entering pillows in the competition. "I just know they're the ones she stole. She couldn't cut them open, so she just sewed covers for them. I'll bet you anything that's what she did."

Mrs. Peppel was, as usual, remarkably calm. "Isn't it the most perfect day for the fair? Let's hope it's the same tomorrow, too—a perfect State Fair weekend." Mrs. Peppel was surely the most unusual person Lacey had ever known.

Lacey was excited by the bustle of the fair, more so this year than ever before because she was helping Mrs. Peppel. The crowds grew early and, soon enough, the screams of the coaster riders could be heard across the fairgrounds. The aroma of barbecue and funnel cakes filled the air. It was a grand and wonderful time.

The craft competition was to take place in one of two huge white tents set up for the occasion. One tent was to be used for the livestock show and judging. That's where Lacey and Regina would later visit Hector Rodriguez and his twelve hundred pound steer to wish him luck.

The other tent was for the exhibitors of crafts and flowers. The craft exhibitors' tables were set at one end of the tent in three long rows that ran nearly the entire length of the covered space. There were homemade quilts, embroidered tablecloths, glass etching, woodcarvings, metal sculptures, painted dishes and stained glass, bird houses and weather vanes. There were pillows and paper blossoms.

Mrs. Peppel's table was set up near the center of one of the rows. There were two categories for the crafts – handcrafts and stitchcrafts. Mrs. Peppel fell into the stitchcraft category. Mrs. Carraway's entry would be in hand crafts. Entries would be judged on most creative, finest quality, and most technically difficult. And, finally, the judges would select one winner for "Best in Show."

Lacey and Regina had taken time to walk through the tent to look at all the entries. They had seen Mr. Houseman's

"Bonneted Lady," a magnificent white-tipped scarlet rose, and thought it was the most beautiful rose at the fair…or anywhere.

"Have you found your five thousand pound bull yet?" Lacey teased.

"It's here. I'm sure of it," Regina replied, raising one shoulder as if to shrug off any criticism. "Or maybe it won't come till tomorrow."

Sure enough, there was Mrs. Hollingsworth. She had a table displaying three pillows, just about the size of those that were in the cardboard carton left by the back door of the shop. The pillows were beautifully covered, one in a vivid summer floral, one in brilliant blue velvet with shimmery tassels, and the third in a rich green plaid taffeta. Mrs. Carraway was right, Lacey thought, her sister Olive did do great work. But Lacey knew that if she were able to go over and squeeze them, they would be just exactly as cushy-mushy, easy-pleasy-squeazy as Mrs. Peppel's, because they *were* Mrs. Peppel's.

"Hmmm," said Regina. "Looks like your dear Mrs. Peppel has some tough competition. What have you got to say about that?"

Lacey didn't know what to say. She had a feeling that Mrs. Peppel would not approve of her telling Regina that Mrs. Hollingsworth had stolen the pillows. She didn't always understand Mrs. Peppel, but she was sure Mrs. Peppel always had something in mind that eventually made sense. Still, time was running out. The judging would take place very shortly.

"I'd better get back to our table," was all she finally said to

Regina. "I'll see you later. I hope your dad's barbecue wins," she said with a smile, and off she went.

The tables were set ten feet apart, and Mrs. Hollingsworth's table was three tables away from Mrs. Peppel's. In between were a husband and wife displaying the colorful country quilts they had made, and two brothers whose specialty was leather crafts—ornately engraved belts and boots, fine leather gloves, and cow whips. Lacey didn't know any of these exhibitors, but wished everyone the best of luck.

One of her favorite parts of the fair was meeting new people from different places who did all kinds of different things. When she had stopped by Mrs. Carraway's table, she got to meet Nathan Carraway and found him to be a very friendly and gracious man.

"So you're Lacey Medina," came his cheerful greeting. "I have heard quite a bit about you, young lady. I'm glad to meet you, indeed."

She felt very happy for Mr. and Mrs. Carraway.

Chapter Eleven

MANY PEOPLE WHO shopped at Mrs. Peppel's or knew her from town stopped by to look at her beautiful handwork and to wish her luck, including Samuel Flutey from the hardware store. Lacey minded the table while Mr. Flutey and Mrs. Peppel went for a walkabout.

A short while later, Mrs. Peppel returned, smiling. Miss Tinnery, Barlemarry's librarian, was at the table talking with Lacey and her parents. "Abigail, your helper is doing quite a nice job."

"I couldn't do it without her," said Mrs. Peppel. "She's the best anyone could ask for." Her words made Lacey feel proud.

"Well, this is quite a time," said Lacey's dad. Whistles and bells from the arcade area outside mixed with the carousel's calliope melodies and the din of gathering crowds.

Jason came by, looking well groomed and sheepish. "Hey," was all he had to say. He kept looking over his shoulder at the pretty girl with the long black hair who kept looking over her shoulder right back at him.

"You're looking quite handsome, Jason," Mrs. Peppel said. Jason put his head down, embarrassed, and poked the pavement with his toe.

"Now don't let her get away," said Miss Tinnery. "She's got her eye on you." With that, Jason grinned slightly, looked over his shoulder again, then slowly headed in that direction.

Lacey's mom went behind the table and stood close to Mrs. Peppel. "I can't believe Olive Hollingsworth is here," she said. "And she's showing pillows? What's that all about?"

"Yes, lovely pillows, aren't they?" was all Mrs. Peppel said about it, then added, "I'm happy to see you both. Your daughter has been a great asset. Thank you so much for allowing her to help at the shop. I'll miss her when school starts."

"She's special to us, too, Mrs. Peppel," said Lacey's dad. "So, thanks for teaching her."

If they only knew the half of it, Lacey thought. And she really did wonder many times over these weeks what they would have thought if they knew about the cloud filler and the thread that couldn't be cut and the fabric that couldn't tear and all the high drama of stolen pillows. Lacey figured that part of growing up was not telling everything you knew just because you knew it, and to hold fast to your promises and responsibilities.

One of the competition coordinators came by, announcing that the judges were in the tent.

"Here you go," said Lacey's dad. "We'd better step away and give you space. Good luck."

Lacey looked down the row of tables and saw Mrs. Hollingsworth. She knew they could prove Mrs. Hollingsworth had stolen the pillows. She still couldn't figure out why Mrs. Peppel wouldn't say anything.

Mrs. Peppel had stopped by Mrs. Hollingsworth's table a short time earlier. "Your pillows are quite lovely, Mrs. Hollingsworth," she said. "I'm sure if the judges were to see them, they would certainly agree."

"What do you mean *if* the judges were to see them," Mrs. Hollingsworth snapped. "They're going to see them, all right."

Then, Mrs. Peppel wished her luck and returned to her own table.

The judges were making their way through the rows, here and there stopping to take a closer look at the workmanship and detail, evaluating the overall quality of the exhibits.

Lacey's heart raced. She knew that winning wasn't important to Mrs. Peppel. She was just happy to be part of this wonderful experience for the first time. What bothered Lacey was possibly seeing Mrs. Hollingsworth win using Mrs. Peppel's very own pillows. Why wouldn't Mrs. Peppel speak up. All she had to do was insist that they open the pillow covers. The evidence was right there, but Mrs. Peppel just smiled and told Lacey to enjoy the beautiful day.

The judges were walking their row now. They would get to Mrs. Hollingsworth's table first, and the smug look that Lacey saw on her face told her that Mrs. Hollingsworth felt very confident about her entries. Her pillows were colorful and plump. She had done an excellent job of covering what she had stolen.

Suddenly, there was a frightening sound. A heavy grumbling shook all the nearby tables. The exhibitors and judges looked around, startled by what was happening. The noise and the shaking were greatest at Mrs. Hollingsworth's table. Her pillows had begun to swell, like over-inflated balloons. They started rolling about.

No one knew what was happening, least of all Mrs. Hollingsworth, who saw her beautiful pillows growing before her eyes, and moving as if alive. Everyone backed away, staring in disbelief. A moment later, there was a near-deafening boom, like the roar of thunder. To everyone's amazement, Mrs. Hollingsworth's pillows blew apart and gushed water onto the table and floor, drenching Mrs. Hollingsworth, as well. And as quickly as it had all happened, it all stopped.

Everyone looked in stunned silence at the limp pieces of soaked fabric that lay in rags across Mrs. Hollingsworth's table. A crowd gathered and people buzzed about what might have caused it, but no one could figure it out. The judges scratched their heads curiously, but finally had to move on to other tables.

Security asked a few questions and chalked it up to some unidentifiable imperfection in Mrs. Hollingsworth's handiwork.

Maintenance arrived quickly and mopped up the mess, gathering all of the pillow fragments into a trash bin—all but one, that is. There was one piece that Mrs. Peppel picked up off the floor. Beneath the once lovely pillow cover that Mrs. Hollingsworth had fashioned, wet as it was, there was that unmistakable piece of piping braided like Lacey's hair.

Mrs. Hollingsworth gasped and threw her hand to her mouth. Lacey saw Mrs. Peppel smile at Mrs. Hollingsworth with that knowing look of hers. Then Lacey and Mrs. Peppel returned to their table just as the judges were examining her pillows. After a few moments, they jotted their notes, nodded, and moved along to the next table.

Lacey looked over at Mrs. Hollingsworth and somehow felt very sorry for her. Her hair and dress were a mess, and she appeared to be near tears as she folded up her table covering. Onlookers hung around, still wondering what had gone wrong, but no one approached Mrs. Hollingsworth.

Any thought Lacey had had about seeing Mrs. Hollingsworth punished now mattered very little. This seemed to be punishment enough. Lacey recalled the conversation she'd had with her mom, talking about Mrs. Hollingsworth and why people are mean. Her mom had said that sometimes people who act mean have been hurt. She remembered what Mrs. Carraway said about her sister and the hard times she had had raising a daughter by herself.

Lacey's dad once told her that a sign of maturity was being able to look more deeply at who people are and why they do the things they do. There was a time when Lacey might have thought that what just happened to Mrs. Hollingsworth was funny. She might have been glad that Mrs. Hollingsworth got what was coming to her. But that's how a child would behave. Lacey never felt less like a child than she did right now.

She walked over to her table. "I'm sorry Mrs. Hollingsworth. Your pillows were beautiful."

Mrs. Hollingsworth slowly folded the table cover. She didn't look up. Lacey picked up one corner of the cloth and folded it toward the middle. Mrs. Hollingsworth gave a quick nod, but still said nothing.

"Is there anything I can do to help you?" Lacey asked.

"You can go away, please," she said quietly. "Just go away." It was not Mrs. Hollingsworth's typical harsh tone. Her voice was soft and sad.

Lacey had never seen Mrs. Hollingsworth like this. She realized how humiliated she must be feeling. Lacey returned to Mrs. Peppel's table, still puzzling like everyone else about what could possibly have caused the pillows to explode. Who had ever heard of such a thing? She had seen the patch of fabric that Mrs. Peppel picked up with the braided piping. There was no question they were Mrs. Peppel's pillows, but what on earth could have…could have…"

Lacey gasped. She knew! Of course! She knew! She slowly looked up at Mrs. Peppel. "Cumulonimbus!" she said in a loud whisper. "You filled them with Cumulonimbus clouds! Storm clouds!"

"I must admit I did," said Mrs. Peppel.

"But how did you know Mrs. Hollingsworth would take the carton?" Lacey asked, still in disbelief.

"I didn't know for sure," Mrs. Peppel said with a shrug. "I could only guess that she might, the way she'd been hanging around the shop all week."

"Are you going to tell the police?"

"Oh, no. No," said Mrs. Peppel. "I have something better in mind." Then she took the piece of torn wet fabric with the piping braided like Lacey's hair and walked over to Mrs. Hollingsworth's table, where the two women had a long talk.

Chapter Twelve

THE REST OF that summer went by quickly. Lacey and Regina made the most of it, hanging out together as often as possible. Regina's birthday was in August and she had a big party with lots of school friends. Mr. Strobel served his now famous barbecue, having finally taken first place at the State Fair.

Lacey continued to enjoy working for Mrs. Peppel two afternoons a week and going up to the bell tower with her. The shop was even busier now that Mrs. Peppel got her blue ribbon. And Regina was beginning to see Mrs. Peppel in a different light.

"Okay, so maybe she's not crazy, just a little weird," said Regina one day. Lacey had explained as best she could about Seraphim, the cat, and the saucer of milk, without giving away any secrets.

Regina was not yet convinced. "There's still that whole peacock thing."

"Why don't you ask her about it," Lacey said. "She doesn't bite, you know."

Regina did just that.

"Ah, yes," said Mrs. Peppel. "Angelorum. That's his name. He's a lovely peacock. White peacocks are rare, you know."

Regina hadn't heard anything about the peacock being white or rare. And she had no idea it was a "he." It all sounded pretty cool. She loved the name *Angelorum*. If she ever got another cat, she would name it that.

"How did you get it?" She asked.

"An old friend of my late husband is with the Dublin Zoo. He came over from Ireland to transport Angelorum from the zoo at Chestnut Springs to the Dublin Zoo. Do you know that the Dublin Zoo was started in 1830?" Mrs. Peppel gave a satisfied sigh. "Anyway, Martin—that's our friend's name—became ill and had to spend a couple of days at the Barlemarry Medical Center. So, he left Angelorum with me. It was a delight having him here. I made a collar for him out of one of my feather gloves and was able to attach one of Ducky's old leashes to it. Angelorum didn't like it at first, but he got used to it pretty quickly. We never stayed out long or went very far. We just took a few short strolls along the preserve near my cottage." And that was the end of that.

Mrs. Carraway's shop also benefitted from the fair. She took the ribbon for "Best in Show," and now the orders poured in for her handmade paper flowers, especially from wedding parties who loved the idea of keeping their bouquets long after the wedding. She surprised Lacey with a special bouquet made just for her.

"None of this would have happened without you, none of it," she told Lacey. "Thank you for all your encouragement. Thank you. Thank you."

As predicted, Mr. Houseman's "Bonneted Lady" was everyone's favorite rose. And as was his custom after winning, he took his precious flower and his blue ribbon to the cemetery and laid them on Mrs. Houseman's grave.

Hector Rodriguez did not win for best steer, but he had made such a strong positive impression on the local farmers that the Barlemarry Cattleman's Association awarded him a full scholarship to the agricultural college in Chestnut Springs. To Lacey's mind, it was a great summer in Barlemarry. She knew, of course, that it was not great for everyone.

Olive Hollingsworth stayed away from town as much as possible. Very few people saw her after the fair. The catastrophe of her exploding pillows had made all the papers, as well as the six o'clock news, and continued to be a puzzle to all and an endless embarrassment to Mrs. Hollingsworth. Once school started, however, she was back in the classroom, and Lacey was the first to notice a difference.

"Didn't you see it?" Lacey asked Regina, as they walked home following their first day of classes.

"See what?"

"Mrs. Hollingsworth. The way she's acting," said Lacey. "She didn't call anyone names. Not once."

"She's probably just getting warmed up," Regina said.

But that wasn't the case. Soon, everyone could see that, day by day, Mrs. Hollingsworth was becoming increasingly... well...civil.

"Is that possible?" Regina asked Lacey. "Can somebody like her actually turn nice? I mean she's not gushing with kindness or anything, but she just doesn't seem to be so cruel."

"Anything is possible," said Lacey, speaking from a whole summer's worth of first-hand experience. Lacey wondered if

Mrs. Hollingsworth's behavior had anything to do with what Mrs. Peppel said to her that day at the fair. Mrs. Peppel had never told Lacey about their conversation. One afternoon in the workroom, Lacey brought it up.

"Mrs. Hollingsworth is acting different this year," she said.

Mrs. Peppel was at the corner shelves, straightening spools of thread. "Different how?"

"Well, she's almost…nice," Lacey said, fidgeting with a piece of velvet fabric.

"What is it you want to ask me, Lacey?"

Lacey never understood how Mrs. Peppel always knew more than should be possible for her to know.

"I was just wondering."

"About our conversation?"

"Yes. Is it a secret?"

"Yes, it is," said Mrs. Peppel, "but not one I would keep from you. You've proven to be very responsible with our secrets." Lacey felt good that Mrs. Peppel trusted in her growing maturity.

Mrs. Peppel turned around and faced Lacey. "When I went over to her table, she saw that I had the piece of torn fabric. I could see she was worried. She asked if I was going to report her to the police. She said it would ruin her career as a teacher. She was quite humbled and told me how very sorry she was for doing such a mean and foolish thing. I felt sorry for her – the way you did."

"What did you tell her?"

"I told her that I had no intention of reporting her or ruining her career as long as she did one thing."

"One thing?"

"Yes, just one thing," Mrs. Peppel said with a shrug.

"What was it?" It seemed to Lacey that when she was around Mrs. Peppel, there was just no end to mystery or surprise.

"I told her that all she had to do was to try to be nice." Mrs. Peppel sighed. "And in the meantime, I would hold onto that piece of fabric."

With the start of the new school year, it was clear that Mrs. Hollingsworth was holding up her end of the bargain. As the weeks passed, she actually smiled at her students. At first, the students found it hard to trust her. They couldn't be sure that she wouldn't suddenly turn on them. But she never did. Lacey knew she wouldn't because she believed Mrs. Hollingsworth had changed. The events of that summer had changed them both.

Mrs. Hollingsworth now listened with respect and complimented them. She corrected them in a kind and civil manner. If, on occasion, she said something that she was afraid the students might interpret as being too harsh, she apologized.

Before long, the students could see she was sincere. Faculty members saw it, too, because she was nicer to them, as well. In fact, she was nicer to everyone. As it turned out, the change was remarkable, but it was not one-sided. The nicer Mrs. Hollingsworth was, the nicer people were to her in return.

The students no longer made fun of her. When her

November birthday rolled around, Lacey and Regina hung balloons in the classroom, and for the very first time Mrs. Hollingsworth did not complain about them. Alyson Chin brought in a small potted fern for her desk, and Philip Runcey led the class in singing the birthday song – all of which brought tears to Mrs. Hollingsworth's eyes. They were happy changes, indeed.

But perhaps the happiest change of all occurred on the Saturday just before Christmas when Lacey was helping out at Mrs. Peppel's. The shop bustled with people selecting favorite pillows to give as gifts. Lacey was behind the counter with Mrs. Peppel to help gift-wrap. It had been such a busy day that neither of them looked up when the bell rang again over the front door.

A few moments later, they were aware that two women were standing at the counter in front of them. They looked up to find a woman they hardly recognized. It was Mrs. Hollingsworth with a smile as wide as all Barlemarry. Her eyes sparkled and when she greeted them her voice was almost musical.

"Oh, Mrs. Hollingsworth," said Mrs. Peppel in her warmest tone, "it is so very good to see you again."

"Likewise, Mrs. Peppel. And you, too, Lacey." Then she gestured to the young woman with her. "I'd like you both to meet my daughter, Evelyn."

It was a brief but joyous visit. Evelyn Hollingsworth proved to be as charming as her newly transformed mother. Evelyn was to be married in the spring and was thrilled that her mom would be making her wedding dress.

"Could I please have a word with you, Mrs. Peppel?" Mrs. Hollingsworth asked. "I know you're busy. I promise to take only a minute of your time."

"Of course," said Mrs. Peppel, as the two of them stepped away.

Mrs. Hollingsworth took Mrs. Peppel's hand. "I would like you to make two white satin-covered bed pillows for my daughter. I want to give them to her as a wedding gift. I want them to be the best; that's why I'd like it very much if you made them."

"I would be honored to make them, Mrs. Hollingsworth."

"Please. Call me Olive."

"Thank you, Olive. Call me Abigail. And speaking of gifts, I have a little something for you."

Lacey was having a pleasant conversation with Evelyn, but noticed Mrs. Peppel looking her way. Lacey gave a nod and went into the workroom. A few moments later, she returned with a small brown envelope and handed it to Mrs. Peppel, who in turn handed it to Olive Hollingsworth.

The two women hugged, then Mrs. Hollingsworth left with her daughter on her arm, and in her purse a small brown envelope containing a piece of torn fabric and a length of piping braided like Lacey's hair.

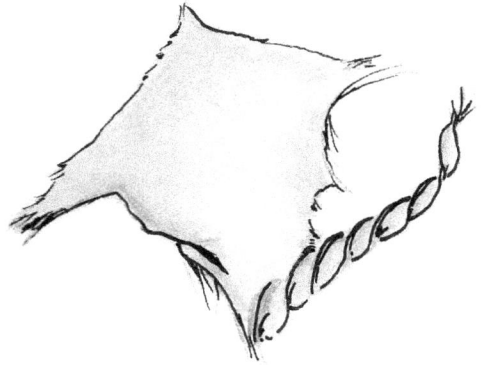

The End